I am Kipper

Written by Roderick Hunt

Illustrated by Nick Schon,
based on the original characters
created by Alex Brychta

OXFORD

UNIVERSITY PRESS

Read our names

I am Kipper.

I am Pam.

I am Mat.

I am Pat.

I am Tom.

I am Mac.

I am Sam.

Sam

Pat Mat

Mac

Kipper Tom

Pam

Missing letters

Choose the letter to make the word.

_____ op

_____ op

_____ ap

_____ op

Talk about the story

Where was Sam?

What was Pam doing?

What were the children dressed up as?

What kinds of games do you play with your friends?

Who did what?

Match each child with the right word.

tap

mop

hop

pop

15

The
Dog Tag

Written by Roderick Hunt

Illustrated by Nick Schon,
based on the original characters
created by Alex Brychta

OXFORD
UNIVERSITY PRESS

Read these words

got

cat

top

cap

pot

mat

mop

tag

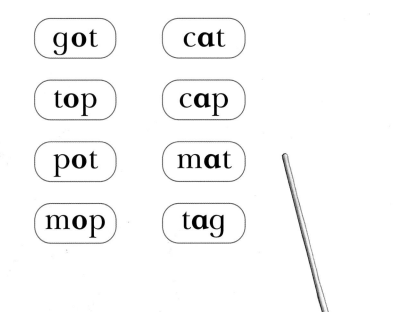

Kipper got a cat.

Biff got a top.

Chip got a cap.

Mum got a pot.

Dad got a mop.

Floppy got a mat.

Floppy got a tag.

Floppy sat on the mat . . .

. . . and he got a pat.

Missing letters

Choose the letter to finish the word.

ca__

ca__

mo__

ta__

Talk about the story

Rhyming pairs

Say the words. Find pairs of words that rhyme.

top

mat

cat

mop

A maze

Help Kipper to get to Floppy.